This is Weird

by PATTY WOLCOTT
Pictures by NICOLE RUBEL

SCHOLASTIC INC.
New York Toronto London Auckland Sydney

ISBN 0-590-33934-6

12 11 10 9 8 7 6 5 4 3 2 1   3   6 7 8 9/8 0 1/9

Printed in the U.S.A.   08

This is the key to the kingdom.

The Kingdom

The Kingdom

The
Key
To
The
Kingdom

In the kingdom,

there is a city.

In the city,

there is a street.

In the street is a yard.

In the house there is a room.

In the room there is a trapdoor.

Under the trapdoor is a tunnel.

Danger
Falling
Rocks

In the tunnel there is
a ghost!

Ghost in the tunnel.
Tunnel under the trapdoor.

Danger
Falling
Rocks

Trapdoor in the room.
Room in the house.

**House in the yard.
Yard in the street.**

Street in the city.

City in the kingdom.

The
Key
To
The
Kingdom

This is the key to the kingdom.